Peedum

…and other original Jamaican village stories.

Lena Joy Rose

minna
PRESS

 Published in Jamaica by Minna Press
204 Mountain View Avenue, Kingston 6, Jamaica W.I.

NATIONAL LIBRARY OF JAMAICA
CATALOGUING-IN-PUBLICATION DATA
Rose, Lena Joy
   Peedum – and other original Jamaican village stories / Lena Joy Rose

   p. : ill. ; cm.

ISBN 978-976-95510-1-5 (pbk)

1. Jamaican fiction   2. Jamaica – Social life and customs   I. Title

813 - dc 22

Cover artwork by Aeron Cargill

Book design by Mark Steven Weinberger

Printed in Tennessee, U.S.A.

DEDICATION

To my sons: Andre & Marc

and to
Jamaican villages…
the communities that inspire heartfelt stories.

A people without the knowledge of their past history, origin and culture is like a tree without roots.

— MARCUS GARVEY

PREFACE

In these short stories and vignettes, I reminisce about my life in a Jamaican village. Names have been changed for obvious reasons.

Strong elements of revivalism and religion permeate my stories as do superstition, African references and customs. These influences can be attributed to the proximity of Watt Town and Clarksonville—villages in the Dry Harbor Mountains of Jamaica.

Watt Town is the birthplace of revivalism in Jamaica and it is still a mecca for revivalists island-wide. Another neighboring village, Clarksonville, was one of the first free villages for ex-slaves after emancipation in 1838.

A few stories extend to life abroad. They underscore that the village we come from nurtures who we are and what we become—no matter where we go. There is an old Jamaican saying that holds true for me: *You can tek de person out a de bush, but you cyaan tek de bush out a de person.*

I hope you enjoy reading these stories as much as I enjoyed excavating them. Please refer to the glossary on page 108, for an explanation of Jamaican words and phrases used in this book.

— LENA JOY ROSE

CONTENTS

My Big Day

Why is the driver playing that ridiculous tune; doesn't he realize that dead people like melodious music too? Even the palm trees swaying in the breeze try in vain to keep time with these tuneless chimes.

Now what in heaven's name could be slowing this hearse? Oh, I see, the entire village folks are lining the streets. They are here just to gawk.

There's Miss Mabel, with tears running down her cheeks. A real hypocrite she is, after she stole my chickens. There's two-faced Jim, looking all pious; I guarantee that by tomorrow he'll say: "Poor soul, she hardly had any flowers on her casket." If the fool went to church, he would know the donations are going for a new church organ and to fix the windows.

All these sweaty faces slide and twist so grotesquely against the hearse's window trying to get a glimpse of my coffin. If they are expecting to see a ghost in here, they should look at themselves. Look at Miss Liz's grandson, his face squashing against the glass. It's the worst—his left lower eyelid stretches way down to his cheekbones, his lips flip over and twist to the right of his nose. Ug-ly!

Listen to what's going on down the street. I tell you some people have no respect. Today is my funeral and the reggae beat is thump, thump, thumping away at Bertie's Rum Bar. At least he turned down the sound.

Thank goodness the hearse is pulling away from the gawkers now. I wish I could peek to see who sent me this beautiful wreath adorning my casket; the air is so thick with the scent of hibiscus and honeysuckle. I bet it came from Miss Liz—she had promised to plant some in my garden. It was always "soon come," so now she's trying to make amends.

I can tell we are now at the church, for the blooming Poinciana trees surround the hearse with a burst of orange brilliance. The branches dip in the breeze, gently tapping the window as a signal for us to stop.

My, my, the street looks like a parking lot! I can't believe all this is for me. Even the police sergeant from High Town is here directing traffic. I hope long-necked Josephine is taking note of all this. I let her know a long time ago that I am someone to be reckoned with, now she will see. She is the one person that didn't show up but I'm sure she's craning her neck from her verandah.

The church is packed with people, fanning themselves with their programs. I'm going to have to take a look at the program later to see what picture they put on the front. I hope it's not my passport picture.

Wait. Who is doing that cow bawling in the front row?

"Maw…maw." It sounds just like Miss Hettie Smith's cow when her calf disappeared down the sinkhole.

Bless me Jesus, if it's not Clarence my first born—the great philosopher doing the bawling. Heh…wasn't he the one who stood at my bedside last week and said to my other kids: "Don't cry guys, there is a time to live and a time to die…when they are old like this you have to expect anything."

I was still alive when he said that too.

Who in the world told him I was ready to die? I still had a lot of plans for my life. He conveniently forgot the rest of Ecclesiastics, which said: "There is a time to weep...there is a time to mourn." If my mouth wasn't locked shut, I surely would have given him a piece of my mind. Why do people think that if you can't speak, then you can't hear?

I have learned more in this last week than I did in my entire seventy-seven years with my mouth going a mile a minute—just listening, observing and digesting things in my mind. For instance, Miss Judy, on her way to the airport, stopped in to say goodbye. She thought she could fool me when she leaned over the bed and whispered in my ear: "Hold on Mama, I'll be coming back in two weeks to take you back to the States with me for rehab." Rehab my foot!

Didn't she think I saw the hopelessness in her eyes? She never looked me in the eye while she was saying those words. I knew it was over for me when I saw her eyes glisten with unshed tears, her bottom lip puckered and pouted further than the top lip, just like when she was little and Janet poked out the eyes of her doll.

Come to think of it, I am lying here just like a rag doll. Some strange man dressed me this morning. What kills me is that he didn't even do a good job. I am certainly not looking my best. It is a terrible thing to be helpless. Imagine, not one of my daughters would search for my new spectacles for me to wear on my big day. No sirree, they were too busy "titivating" themselves with their fancy clothes. And my poor wash belly, Guthrie, she can't even dress well. I pray she isn't wearing the same tight dress she wore to Uncle Lester's funeral last year—the back was hiking up in the air. The front looked like she was having body come down.

Oh what is this now? As God liveth, I can't even kiss my teeth in disgust. I bet my false teeth are still floating in the glass on my chifforobe. I hope a fly don't drop in the glass for that's one thing I can't stomach.

Here come a sea of faces, in every shade of brown imaginable, washing over me, ebbing and flowing like Rio Cobre after hurricane Gilbert. Merciful Redeemer, they leave in their wake wafts of Khus Khus, Charlie, Jontue, Halston and Youth Dew; mixed with their sweat. Egad! I am nauseous.

Wait a minute; let me hear what these people have to say about me. Who is that up in the pew? Oh, it's Brother Percy. He is so choked with emotion I can barely hear him saying "...a good woman, a kind woman, I remember when she met Brother Jasper at Miss Iris' wedding they became inseparable after that."

Yes all that's true, but Jasper is the one who chased me straight into matrimony. Look at him now poor thing. Heh, heh, life is just like a game of cards—you don't know when you'll hold the Joker. Who would have thought that after thirty years of nursing Jasper from prostate cancer, lung cancer, scarlet fever, and pneumonia...he would be the one, at 92 years of age, to put me in the grave? I got high blood pressure from worrying over his ailments.

I am so glad that neither he nor the rest of the kids listened when the philosopher suggested: "Make it a double grave, so when Dada goes we can just put him on top."

On top of who?

Can you imagine after 60 years of married life and bearing eight children, I should journey into eternity with a man riding on top of me?

Shucks, it's about time I get my own space. After all.

Everyone's going for communion now. I love the Anglican Church. Such a sense of peace and holiness. I tell you, this is so much classier than the ruckus they've been making in my yard for nine-night. I've been fit to be tied! I don't harbor that kind of yagga-yagga music in my yard. Bongo drums. Calabash. Guitar. Tambourines. Mouth Organ and all kinds of electronic music. Lord have mercy on me.

The worst was when the truck came. The only time an open back truck ever pulled up in my yard was when Marse Norman came to deliver my cylinder of gas. Now this truck was filled with "dead-yard singers," probably from Watt Town. They hopped out of the back like cop-cop ants, scrambling up to my yard in single file, beating their tambourines, their heads tied with red turbans like they're running duppy.

The singing was another matter. Peg-leg Sammy, with his one foot, marched up and down the crowd of people, commandeering the songs. He weaved in and out like he was playing mauly charly. Where they got all those chairs from to sprawl out on the lawn beats me. Some people played dominoes while others sat, swaying and singing. Who appointed Peg-leg chairman of the nine-night? He and I were never companions. When Peg-leg wailed some nonsense, the crowd chanted right behind him. I've never seen nothing like that in a sankey book. Everything he said, they repeated in song, dragging out every syllable and every word. My God, it sounded so mournful, echoing off the hilltop and beyond. It tugged at my heartstring and almost moved me to tears.

And when Peg-leg fling his one good foot out, belching out a song, "who ha de key for Mass Jasper room," I couldn't believe the people started to sing it too. When they wanted food they sang for the food. When they wanted rum… I tell you it was a mockery. That was when I flew in a temper and dropped the dutchie on Miss Liz's foot. I didn't mean for it to hit her. It was Peg-leg's good foot I was aiming at, so he'd sit down and shut up.

I was disappointed that all my pickney them, who I have kept away from all this, would sanction this charade. I heard one explaining to her foreign husband that "the nine-night is a traditional ritual at most Jamaican funerals in the country and it is reminiscent of our tribal, African roots." She favor puss jook. I don't know when since she decide to come from Africa when is right here she born. Right here me born. Right here my mother born, and my mother mother and her mother, mother, mother! And anything before that don't count.

To make matters even worse, a few men started a Dinki Mini. If I had known I would have saved throwing the dutch pot until then. One heap of foolishness! They danced and gyrated their hips balancing cotta sticks on their heads; they beat condensed cans with sticks, tamboos and scratched bent-up graters with nails. I just sucked my teeth when I overheard the next explanation, all this intellectualizing, to the foreign husband: "See? This is straight from a tribe in Africa, I forgot the name, but the idea is to defy the death that has occurred. By gyrating the pelvic area they are proving they are more powerful than death as they have the means to reproduce."

My heart started to roost from my chest at the clinical tone, as if my passing is related to anthro whatever she had decided to study. The degree she couldn't get a job with. All they do is dig into people's business and when they're not satisfied, they dig into people's mother and their mother's-mother's business.

What the devil my passing has to do with cotta and grater? God ye knows. Imagine, she should be mourning for her mother but no, she's too busy, Miss Crips-Crips, trying to impress with her knowledge. That's what I sent her to university for, spent up my money—for her to go and learn about Quashie?

To cool down my temper, I went for a stroll in the moonlight. The night breeze felt so good on my skin as I pondered my new state of being. I relished the peace away from all those people, chatting and singing songs that were never in my acts of worship. Then I heard the scream.

"Duppy! Duppy! Look back-a-tank, look, look," a little boy we called Peadove pointed, startling me out of my ruminations. I ducked behind the star apple tree and was amazed at how easily I could merge as one with the tree. Peadove's grandmother came out of the kitchen and cuffed him on the back of his bald head. "Nutten no go so. You too lie—go inside and watch TV with the other pickney them."

She returned to stoking the fire underneath the big kerosene pan filled with mannish water. As the aroma wafted below my nostrils, all the mawga dogs in Bamboo Grove Village decided to gallop through the corn piece like horses at Caymanas Park. Miss Liza's fool-fool dog skidded to a halt while the others raced by. The stupid dog rocked back on its haunches, staring at me with eyes full of donkey matter and started to howl.

As long as the night was I never shut my eyes. Not even for a minute. This was a first. I was awake for my own "set-up" night, even when the dog got hoarse and left me still glued to the star apple tree trunk. It was not the dog. It was not the moonlit night. It wasn't even the bang-a-rang going on in my yard. The easiest way to describe what was going on with me is to say, I felt like I was in one of those fool-fool paintings that Judy dragged me to see in Manhattan—the painting called, *Egg on a Plate Without a Plate.*

Today, I'm so glad that out-of-body experience is over. I feel very grounded now and filled with purpose. A sense of calm overtakes me as I face my big day. I beam with pride as I see all my kids in the church. They sure make me proud. Look what I have produced. Even Judy is dressed for the occasion.

Ha! I noticed she ran to church last Sunday after she got the news that I was gone. Heh heh, she would never see a church door since she became an adult—no matter how much I begged. But nothing happens before the time. Wow, Donny, he looks like the walking wounded, poor thing. The others look as if a swarm of bees stung them around their eyes.

Tony is taking up the collection. I hope they put plenty money in the plate for the new organ and the stained glass window next to the pulpit because it well want to fix. From the time the bloody baldpate fly into it, the crack's getting bigger and bigger. May the Lord have mercy upon my poor soul. I hope Tony will straighten up and fly right from now on and won't give Judy any more trouble. You know, she didn't take him to church when he was little, so that's what she gets now. Yes sirree. I've always told her: "Whatsoever you sow, that you will reap and if you don't follow in the ways of the Lord—nothing but trouble will come to you."

I know some of my children are just mouthing the words to the last song the congregation is singing: "Nearer my God to thee." No sounds are coming out of their mouths I'm sure.

Good! They should be upset. I've been a wreck looking after all of them when they were little. What I didn't see in life, I am now seeing in death—all the sniping sisters clinging together for support.

Speaking of support though, my church sisters certainly knocked themselves out fixing up the church. When they first rolled me in, the red polished floor nearly blinded me. I wonder who they got to give it such a high shine. And the vestry table. Wow! It's even decked out with the white linen tablecloth Judy and I bought at K-Mart in New Jersey, just before I got sick. The sides seem a little short, but that was the longest one they had.

I hope to God Miss Jess don't decide to traipse off the choir and sing her off-key solo because that would just be the limit. Or, Miss Lyn playing the organ. I swear that woman can't see, and she won't wear her glasses. She'll play to the tune of "Guide Me O Thou Great Jehovah" while everyone sings

"Great is Thy Faithfulness." Thank goodness I don't ever have to suffer that anymore. From now on it's nothing but harp for me!

I know, I know, I'm getting edgy. I wish they would just hurry up and wrap up all this pomp and ceremony. The good Lord knows I am weary. I have been cooped up for two long months being poked with needles, getting brain scan, lung scan; people twisting me here, pulling me there. When your time is done here, if you don't already know it in your mind, your body will surely tell you.

Aaah, at last. Miss Lyn is playing the right tune with the right song. This is highly irregular. She's never played so well before. Never. This must be for my benefit. I take it as a sign that God is bestowing his favor on me. A prelude of the synchronicity that awaits me in HIS arms. All of a sudden, joy just unfurls and bursts through my chest like a daffodil. I hear the strains of the melody and feel it seeping into my very soul:

> *Swing low, sweet chariot,*
> *Coming for to carry me home,*
> *Swing low, sweet chariot,*
> *Coming for to carry me home.*
> *I looked over Jordan, and what did I see?*
> *Coming for to carry me home.*

Yep, that's right. My dear sons and sons-in-law are carrying my coffin out of the church—marching as if they each have two wooden left feet. They pause by the steps outside and the air is still, except for the blue-tailed hummingbirds. The welcoming sun singes the tip of my nose as I face the wide open canvas of a sky. I could just kick up my heels, fling my arms in the air and shout like Martin Luther King: "Free at last, free at last, thank God Almighty, I'm free at last."

Literary Festival Award Winner, 2010
Jamaica Cultural Development Commission (JCDC)

Abide With Me

On Ash Wednesday, late evening, I squalled into this world—amidst a fanfare of steel-drummed calypso music, jonkoono dancing and rum-swigging cheers. Or so I'd like to imagine. According to reports from various family members, the first part is correct; I squalled straight through babyhood. To my parents—that must have been a major irritation. Indeed, I don't recall any of those years. What I do recall are fondest memories of my grandmother.

Before I found her lying on the floor one early morning, she and Aunt B had been my refuge. Not so much Aunt B but my grandmother Na-Na. Where she got that name is a mystery.

Why was "out-a-yard" as we called Na-Na and Miss B's house a refuge for me? It was a place to play—to be me without the ever watchful eyes of Mama. A place to escape whippings and the mind-numbing routines—the endless cleaning, sweeping up yard every morning, washing on Monday, ironing on Tuesday, tripe soup on Friday and such.

I think I was born knowing how to read or I taught myself with Na-Na's help. I read parts of the bible for her. She'd say her "eyes were dim" and couldn't make out the words. So by lamplight I'd read, and spell what I didn't know. The stories fascinated me as they transported me to another time and place. My favorites were:

"And Ruth said, "Entreat me not to leave thee, or to return from following after thee: for whither thou goest, I will go; and where thou lodgest, I will lodge: thy people shall be my people and thy God my God...."

Then Na-Na would explain that this verse showed Ruth's loyalty and that it was a good trait for little girls to have too.

"And the meek shall inherit the earth...."

Don't be a show off.

"Cast thy bread upon the water for thou shalt find it after many days...."

Whatever you give will come back to you.

"What you sow, you shall reap."

If you plant bad seeds you'll reap a bad crop. Whatever you put in that's what you get out.

Then there were the Pharaoh stories, King Herod, Saul, Jonah and the Whale, Moses and the Burning Bush, Adam and Eve, David and Goliath. Lot's wife and the pillar of salt—all of the Old Testament with their miraculous stories teaching willingness of spirit, obedience, gratitude and love. The bible sustained me for a while. I believed in it unconditionally. One sultry day I walked down the dirt path, lined with coffee and orange trees, leading to Na-Na's house. I looked up into the sky and nestled between two floating clouds was the head of Jesus looking down at me, his hands clasped in prayer. Na-Na said I saw Him because I'm blessed.

Soon after, everything changed. One morning I got up unusually early with a strong inexplicable urge to play with Na-Na. I was six or seven years old. With dew still damp on my feet, I paused at her back door on the concrete piazza. No one was astir. Only "Delicate," Aunt B's three-legged dog raised his head, opened one rheumy eye then lowered his head back down on the step.

I probably would have been chided if I pounded on the door so I skipped over the coffee beans, laid out in a thin row to dry on the piazza. I rummaged around the big stone oven at the side of the house. I could almost picture Na-Na shoving bake-bake on a long wooden pole through the square hole of this oven.

Finally I found a branch that would glide under the door crack—a long enough branch that Na-Na would see or hear scratching the floor while still in bed. I could tease her with it. With determination I placed the branch under the door and swished it back and forth calling softly, "Na-Na is me."

But the branch kept hitting something lying on the floor and no furniture was supposed to be in the way!

Then I heard a low moan.

"Na-Na!" I called out, afraid.

A low moan again.

I ran screaming to the other side of the piazza to pound on the backdoor of Aunt B's bedroom. "Aunt, Aunt, wake up, wake up!"

A bleary-eyed Aunt B, her mouth pursed in annoyance, cracked the door. "Pickney, what you causing such a commotion so early for?"

"Na-Na drop down!" I said, between heaving breaths.

Aunt B's face blanched in shock. She flung the door wide open and I rushed in following her across the hall, her petite frame swallowed by a voluminous nightgown.

We found Na-Na lying flat on her back, on the floor, her head blocking my switch. Na-Na's usually secure headscarf now loped across one eye, revealing mounds of iron gray braids. Not a muscle moved on her body, only that low moan again from her compressed lips. Aunt B called for reinforcements. Everything became a blur to me after that.

It took several days for Na-Na to die.

I was eager to talk to her. She laid on the bed still, a scarf tied loosely around her head, skimming her brows. Her long fingers stretched out at her sides over neatly tucked sheets. I leaned over to check her breathing, but only smelled the whiff of bay-rum she used to ward off head colds. She never turned her head to look at me. She never opened her eyes. She never said a word.

In the dim room, I sat by her bedside with the ruffle-edged curtains drawn. I studied her profile, from her high aquiline nose to her chiseled lips and soft crepe cheeks, wondering if she was dead and I was too late.

Tears welled up clouding my vision. On the dresser, an enamel bowl with uneaten chicken soup swam before my eyes. Framing the dresser's mirror, black and white photos turned askew with Uncle Dave, Aunt Lily, and all of Na-Na's children living in America. A big wardrobe loomed like a dark sentinel against the wall giving off a faint mothball scent.

My eyes roamed the nightstand, flitting over the 'Home Sweet Home' lamp, a bottle of Limacol, a vial of Phensic, to land on the brown, leathered bible. I picked it up and thumbed past the handwritten inscription of my grandmother's name. My fingers moved of their own volition to Psalms 23, her favorite. I smoothed the crumpled ribbon marker down the middle and began to read out loud:

"The Lord is my shepherd I shall not want, he maketh me to lie down in green pastures; he restoreth my soul...."

At the end of the passage, Na-Na's lips moved. "And I will dwell in the house of the Lord forever. Amen." We finished the verse together like we did so many times before. In a voice now barely above a whisper, she told me she'd no longer be with me— she was going to heaven. When I started to cry she reassured me that she'd always be with me.

I didn't believe her. "If you're dead how will I see you?' I asked with a sniff. In mounting alarm I added, "I don't want to see your duppy!"

"No child you won't see me."

"So how will I know you're there then?"

Her lips twitched a half-smile. "When you come to visit my grave," her voice trailed then she continued, "If a little branch dip down and brush your shoulder, it's only me saying hello."

"Are you sure you won't scare me—jump out at me looking like a duppy?"

She shook her head and drifted off to sleep.

I accepted that she was going to die. I felt no

grief—only contentment that she'd always be with me. I decided to get busy. I rounded up all my friends. We found hoes and shovels beneath the house, in the darkened cellar.

Under the shade of a tall breadfruit tree we dug a shallow, rectangular hole in the ground. We filled it with stones, covering the platform with red dirt and freshly picked flowers. As I carefully laid the brilliant red anthuriums in a row on the fresh mound I began to sing:

"Abide with me. Abide with me; fast falls the eventide;

The darkness deepens; Lord with me abide.

When other helpers fail and comforts flee,

Help of the helpless, O abide with me."

The adults in the house heard the singing. When they saw what we did they shooed us away, their faces disturbed.

"What a wicked little gal," said one woman kicking away the stones.

"But Aunt…" I protested. "It's for Na-Na," I tried to explain to the other women in vain. I watched from the corner of the house as they dismantled my altar to Na-Na, breaking the flowers from their long stems, twisting the pink tongues from their center and throwing them in the bushes.

"Don't know what Miss Dorcas going do with her," another said, leveling the mound with her foot.

"Nana still alive and that little wretch ready to

put her in the ground," said a woman as she cut her eyes at me and stalked back up the steps, through the front door.

Na-Na died the next day.

My mother, Miss Di, Miss Dee, Aunt B and the embalmer prepared the body for burial. From my vantage point, sitting on a pile of rocks by the tank, I could see the women passing bucket after bucket of sibble oranges in and out of the back door. I imagine it was to scrub the body the way my mother scrubbed the chicken with sibble orange after she killed it and plucked the feathers each Sunday.

Subdued voices. They finally laid the body out in the living room. I stayed away after that.

The only memory I have of the funeral is a faceless crowd fanning themselves with pleated paper fans. They sang and swayed from side-to-side at the graveside. Aunt Lily, not quite five feet tall, emerged from the throng to commandeer a shovel from the stalwart gravediggers. She braced her feet apart in her hobble skirt and swooped with the shovel, pitching red dirt over the coffin with an energy fueled by grief.

I didn't see Aunt B, my mother, my father or even the mourners who wailed over and over:

"It is well...It is well...with my soul...

With my soul...it is well...it is well with my Soul..."

All I saw in the end was Aunt Lily's spiked-heeled shoes sinking, deeper and deeper in the soft ground as she shoveled dirt.

Months later, my brother Donny and I, with Winsome and Papa-Son, played marbles "out-a-tomb" by the family graveyard. My grandfather's tomb was the favorite as it had high sides so the marbles wouldn't roll away. I was the youngest, so pretty soon they shoved me aside.

I left them and sat near Na-Na's tomb, under the orange tree, watching the game. A branch dipped, the leaves grazing my cheek. There was no breeze. I steadied my racing breath and continued to watch the game. But when the branch dropped, brushing my shoulder like a caress, my heart flipped in my chest. My head started to grow, twice its size, and I could almost hear my grandmother saying... "It's only me saying hello."

The Heat

The heat is not my friend…
It never was…even when I was ten
walking to school with an umbrella over my head
I feared I'd end up brain dead.
I said, the heat is not my friend…

Even when I hydrate
with water starting to percolate
I turn into a living sauna, rivulets of sweat
making tracks down my chest.
I tell you this heat is not my friend…

I set sail for foreign shores—there is nothing better
Until I got the letter…
Come home…
I packed all I own…
Now, I make peace with the heat that was
not my friend…

with a little help from my friends who are
oh so neat:
SPF, shades, wide hat and the hypnotic reggae beat
I look up from the beach toward the sun
And I'm so ready to have some fun!
"Hello heat…I'm here my friend!

Peedum

The month of August felt like eternity for children in the bush; long, sultry, empty days and the best you could do is hope for a miracle to break the tedium. And when you couldn't hope anymore you start to imagine.

We would imagine things that just weren't there.

"Look deh! Look outside. Oh my God!" My brother Donny, who had just turned 12, exclaimed in excitement at dinner.

I'd look and not see anything. My parents had not joined us at the table yet so we had a window of freedom. Donny leaned his lanky frame closer and pointed, "look way up in the tree I can't believe it!" His face took on frightful contortions, his eyes bulging as if he'd seen a duppy.

I'd crane my neck, squinting my eyes to no avail. When I gave up and got back to eating—my favorite chicken leg was gone from my plate. If I continued to search outside for his invisible "thing" long enough I'd miss a chicken wing too. I couldn't do anything about it but fume because he acted innocent, only the exaggerated flare of his long nose gave him away.

After dinner, we filled our bath pans with water and bathed behind the tank. Donny would bathe first. When he was finished he'd call me to view the distinct swirls in the pan. "My bath water looks just like Clarence's water," he'd say.

"How do you know that?" I said, feeling jealous. I had never seen our brother Clarence. He had left the island for England years ago. So Donny would boast that he knew him and saw his bathwater after he bathed.

I couldn't let him get one up on me so after I bathed, I called him, swishing more carbolic soap under the water to form a few swirls and declared. "That's Sister Annie's water!"

He smirked in derision; a brother's bathwater, especially a brother that I'd never seen, was worth more. Even though we had other siblings, we paid homage to the two living in that mysterious place called foreign.

After our baths, we'd play a game of "peedum," a name we made up where we imagined we had bicycles. We'd lay flat on our backs on the bed and put the soles of our feet together in the air and ride. As we coasted along we would sing "peeeeeee" and as we hit an imaginary pothole we would interject the "dum." Suddenly, Donny would ride so fast he'd push me off the bed and cry "peedum!" That usually meant he was tired of humoring me.

Before I went to sleep, I'd dream of riding a brand new bike up and down the street waving to my friends as I sped by. But always, I'd end up playing the stupid game of peedum and yearn that a fairy godmother would wave a wand and grant me all of my wishes. Or that instead of the usual new clothes, I'd get a bike from the magical realm of "farrin."

One Friday morning, Donny and I were "down-a-shop," in front of the house. He was always in charge of looking after me. We played marbles and loafed around. Mr. and Mrs. Jackson drove up in their silver Angler, one of the few families in the small village of Bamboo Grove with a car. Mrs. Jackson alighted, her complexion the color of butter. She wore a brightly flowered dress, with a blue satiny scarf draped over her head, covering her ears and cheeks, and tied loosely under the chin.

"Marse Jasper, how are you and how is Miss Dorcas?" she said unsmiling, holding her little black patent handbag in the crook of her arm.

Papa looked up from his sewing machine, with a big smile, "Oh feeling grand, just grand!" He bobbed his full crop of snowy white hair. He always seemed ancient to me but he carried himself erect, important-looking. Mostly everyone sought his counsel. He and Mrs. Jackson chatted for a while. Mr. Jackson sat quietly in the car resting his head in his hand on the opened window, sometimes speaking, sometimes not.

Mrs. Jackson stepped back on the piazza as if to return to the car and paused. She looked at me all the way down her beaked nose.

"Marse Jasper is this my little god-daughter?" she asked, with some surprise.

"Same one," Papa said. His face beamed as he flicked his wrist for me to stand.

She spun me around.

"She grow eh?"

She clutched her handbag under her arm. "You know I've never given her anything."

I looked at her hopeful. At last, my own fairy godmother to give me a Barbie doll, a new fairy tale book. I glanced over at Donny; he couldn't get the best of me now. I felt special, she chose me.

"What's her name?"

I opened my mouth to reply but Papa gave me a quelling glance before he responded.

"She certainly favors you in looks, Marse Jasper. I'm going to buy a raffle ticket for her when I go to High Town."

Those few words dashed my hopes. Donny sneaked me a "don't know what you expected" look. We went back to playing marbles. Sometimes he'd burst out into involuntary "tee hee" chuckles, sounding like a cat with tisik.

The next Friday a truck pulled up to the front of the house. Soon, shouts of "Judy, Judy, you win de raffle" reached me on the verandah. The shouts came from several children who milled around the shop's piazza.

Donny and I raced down the hill and skidded on the gravel pavement in front of Papa. The truck's engine cranked loud in my ear as Papa ripped off the brown paper wrappings like he was shucking corn. Gasps arose from everyone.

I stared at the burgundy and silver beauty being unveiled before my eyes, hearing from a distance the driver explaining, "Mrs. Jackson…raffle…High Town…winning ticket."

The driver hopped up in his truck, shifted gears and drove off in a cloud of dust. The children ran behind, clinging to the back bumper of the truck, their feet swinging off the road.

I remained rooted to the spot until Papa ripped every scrap of paper from the bicycle. Donny's brown eyes, round with excitement, glanced at me with a "you did something right for a change" look.

Papa never gave us the bicycle; instead he let out his trademark sigh. He didn't do it silent and breathy like everyone else but expelled it loud and long through his parted lips, deep from his gut—haaaigh. His entire chest would rise and fall with the effort.

Papa leaned the bike on the wall of the shop and walked away without a word. We touched its shiny sleekness. It even had a burgundy rubber horn which I squeezed and jumped back.

"It's a fixed wheel," Donny declared knowingly. "You can't ride it—it's not for girls."

"Yes I can too!"

"Well, I'll have to teach you."

He moved the bicycle a few inches, down the length of the wall, glancing out of the corner of his eyes at Papa. Our father studied us for a brief second then refocused on his sewing, pumping the sewing machine with his feet. That meant OK as far as we were concerned.

Donny started to run with my bicycle. I couldn't let him take the first pass at it so I held on to the seat, like a croaking lizard on a beam, while he steered the bicycle on the road.

When we got to Old Post Office he jumped on, pedaling fast.

"It's my turn now, my turn!" I cried, while he zigzagged up to Mrs. McFarlane's gate.

"I tell you, it's a fixed wheel you can't ride it," he said, hopping off to hold it steady for me.

I jumped up on the seat but had to stretch my

legs to reach the pedals. He started to laugh. "You can't ride tip-toe, I'll ride and you can sit in front on the cross bar," he said.

I wasn't too pleased but I relented. Soon we rode around Bamboo Grove Village School in the level area, over the cricket grounds on the left, and where we played soft ball on the right until we circled the big tamarind tree in the school yard. We returned to the street, pulling close to the curb when a car passed by.

"Let me try now."

He jumped off. "Alright I'll hold it while you learn," he said. I marveled at his beneficence.

I figured out if I moved closer to the front of the seat I'd be able to pedal. The seat was uncomfortable but I wouldn't complain and forfeit my right to ride. I started to pedal, and yelled out in pain when the metal pedal hit my ankle as it spun around by itself.

"I told you it was a fixed wheel," Donny mumbled and hissed his teeth.

Finally, I got the hang of it, loving the sound of the chain as I pedaled. Donny walked and held the bike while I rode. He even let go a few times. I proudly pedaled along then circled back to get him. He grinned his approval.

"Let's ride up to Miss Lela's gate and ride down the hill," he suggested.

He jumped behind me and pedaled while I sat on the lower bar and held my legs outstretched in front of me. Halfway up the hill he said, "You're too heavy, get off." I reluctantly hopped down but held on to the seat while I ran behind.

When we arrived at Miss Lela's gate, I sat in front and we rode fast down the hill shouting "wheeeeeeee."

Papa must have heard us. He came out of his shop. "Stay away from the middle of the road!" he shouted for us to hear. We obeyed and stuck close to the curb until he was satisfied and went back to his work. Up the hill we went again. By this time I was tired of riding in the front and wanted to get a taste of the power and speed by myself.

"You can't do it—you might break your neck," Donny argued.

"If you can do it why can't I?"

He sighed. "Alright, I'll push you."

"You mustn't let go though."

"Nah, nah, come on."

He held on to the seat while I rode downhill several times and when I reached the level area I yelled, "let go, let go" and I rode perfectly. I was elated.

We pulled the bike way up on the curb as McCauley's bus tilted dangerously to one side in passing. I was terrified the crocus bags and green bananas on top would topple over on us. I knew when McCauley's passed our house it was almost time for dinner.

"Let's go one more time," I begged.

We raced up the hill again one last time. Donny ran behind me downhill and I rode fast, feeling free, confident, and in control.

I didn't hear him panting behind me.

I glanced over my shoulder. Donny wasn't there.

Alarmed, I turned around. He was left behind, half-way down the hill jumping up in the air, laughing and flailing his arms over his head.

I panicked.

The steering wheel wobbled, my foot slipped and the darned pedal struck me again on the other ankle.

The bicycle fell in the street with an endless clang. I tumbled to the curb, scattering gravel. Humiliation washed over me. My ankles hurt and my knees skinned raw. I lay in the road and started to bawl. Donny ran down to the scene. "Now look what you did," he said picking up the bicycle inspecting it for damage.

"You said you would hold it. I told you don't let go," I wailed.

"No you didn't! You said "let go, let go."

"That was the time before!"

"No it wasn't!"

"Yes it was!"

"Come, come." Papa clapped his hands. "Miss Dorcas's got dinner ready. Donny, bring the bicycle and lean it back where you found it."

"Yes suh!"

"Go up the yard and let your mother put some peroxide on your knee." My ankles had started to swell.

Mama waited for me with the enamel basin filled with cool water. A "strapping woman," my father would proudly say to describe her robust size. As she rinsed my abrasions, I caught the familiar whiff of the light rosewater scent that she splashed on every day. Her heavy-handedness and long-suffering expression more than told me, "it served me right." She promised to dress it after dinner. I didn't look forward to it.

Dinner was tense. I wondered where the bike was and I guessed Donny thought the same as there were no antics at dinner. Maybe he felt some remorse that I fell off the bike. He scraped most of the tripe from his plate to mine. Then he shot me a meaningful, "see how kind I am to you" look.

Mama talked with animated gestures and expressions as she related everything that had gone wrong during the course of her day. Papa listened, bobbing his head in agreement, his face calm. Donny craned his neck looking through the back door for the bike. I hissed under my breath, "You see it?" He shook his head slightly. Mama paused and gave us a long, silent stare.

We couldn't wait to leave the table but we had to wait until Papa finished eating. Finally, he scraped the uneaten scraps neatly to one side of his plate, placing the fork and knife down the center. With a flourish, he splayed his white handkerchief in the air, wiped his lips, cleared his throat and turned his chair to the side, "cutting his ten". That was the signal. Dinner was over.

Jen, a young lady with a wide face, little or no hair, and a secret smile, helped Mama with the household chores. She sashayed her hips into the dining room and cleared away the dishes. I raced outside behind Donny to search for the bike. We looked under the cellar but couldn't find it.

Mama called us for our bath and to dress my knee and rub a foul-smelling liniment on my ankle.

Later, we breathed a sigh of relief when Papa walked the bike into the detached room, the kitchen room, where Mordecai, Papa's helper, slept. Mordecai, in his early twenties, worked the farm and tended the cows, pigs, goats and donkeys. He and Papa hoisted the bicycle up into the ceiling with ropes. "So that no one will steal it overnight," Papa said to no one in particular. But we were satisfied.

We didn't have to play Peedum that night. We had the real thing. Plus we were too preoccupied. Mama sat by the opened living room window to the verandah, listening to a cricket game from her transistor radio. She perched the radio on the window sill for good reception, now and then slapping it hard to remove static.

Mordecai spoke with Papa in low tones on the verandah about the cow-calf, punctuating his discourse with a loud, "Miss Dorcas what's the score?"

Jen hummed tuneless notes while she hemmed her dress in the back bedroom.

Neither Donny nor I slept 'out-a-yard' with Aunt B that night. She quietly came and sat in the big, red armchair next to the bathroom and dozed. She'd sleep with me in the bottom room later but it was not yet nine o'clock.

Donny and I, lying in the middle room, came to a truce. We discussed what we'd do the next day with the bike. He agreed to hold on and run behind while I ride down the hill. I agreed to let him ride the bike, alone, to visit his friends: Mose, Hopeton and Benji. The bike was officially ours.

The next morning I woke up late. Aunt B was long gone. I didn't get much sleep. All night long, cows ready for the slaughter, had bawled piteously into the wee hours. I tossed and turned, alternately marveling about the bike and wondering if the cows knew they only had a few hours before Marse Man-Man, the butcher would come.

Jen knocked on my door. "Your breakfast ready," she called, with affection in her voice.

"What is it?"

"Porridge," she said and giggled.

I groaned, burying my head deep under the pillow. I wouldn't ask what kind, whether it was cornmeal, rice, or worse, banana porridge, all nasty concoctions to me. I decided I'd skip breakfast and pick a big navel orange from the tree in the front yard. It would tide me over until lunch. I remembered the bike and I flew out of bed, changing my clothes. Already the cuts on my knees were ready to scab. I pounded on Donny's door.

"Wha!" he said in a loud, irritated voice. He was never one for early risings but I knew just how I'd get him up.

"I'm going to take the bike for a ride," I said, my voice dripping with molasses.

All of a sudden, rapid stumbling on the wood floor like he was hopping out of his pajamas and his foot got stuck. By the time I got to the back stoop he was there, his cheeks puffed out in his own peculiar glower. We went into the "kitchen room" and looked up in the ceiling with anticipation.

No bike.

"Mordecai, where's the bike?" Donny asked with furrowed brow.

"Heh! Go ask Marse Jasper," he said, bending his head so I couldn't see his expression; only his high cheekbones and noncommittal eyes. We stared after him as he walked the donkey under the clothes line to meet Papa by the willow tree.

"Papa, where's the bike?" I asked with much trepidation.

"Why you're asking me for the bike. Can you eat a bike?" he asked, his voice gruff. His gray hair turned silver in the sunlight.

"No suh!" We shook our heads.

"You want a bike so you can kin puppa lick and break your necks?"

"No suh!" we said together, solemn.

"Well, there's the bike . . ." he said, and pointed.

"Maa-Maa," a bleating sound came from behind us.

We were afraid to look.

"Maa-Maa," louder now.

In slow motion we turned just our necks to see a nanny goat and kid tied to the ackee tree, chomping unconcerned in the grass.

We stood frozen in one spot as the sickening awareness creamed the surface of our minds.

Our bike, replaced by goats.

Papa sighed heavy. He became blurred in my vision as he strolled, his arms hanging out from his sides, toward Mordecai and the donkey. Mordecai's eyes, laced with sympathy, peered at us over the donkey's hamper.

Donny and I stood ignited with loss like two long fire sticks that glowed in the outdoor hearth. We looked at each other, tears washing down our cheeks. No sound. Only a silent communication seemed to pass between us— a vow, unspoken.

We never played peedum again.

Small Up Yourself

I ride in a mini-bus pell knell
down Queens Highway
Speeding
Overtaking
Cutting in and out
Stopping short to pick up one more.
They read the disinterested gazes
the shrugs and impassive faces
to find the ones going their way.
And when they do
it's time to take out the jumpseat
"Small up Yourself, Small up Yourself"
the conductor commands, the passengers grumble.
He turns a dagger stare "You slim lady sit forward."
They shuffle in their seats, until they sit on one butt
cheek.
Then we're off, down Queens Highway
Listening to the scratchy CD player blaring
"My Redeemer Lives."

Thru de Night

"It won't work if you don't take off your blouse," I said, giving my friend Muncie a shove. "You have to be naked to your waist."

"What do you want me to do with all this leaf-a-life?" Janet my other friend said holding her dress front filled with green, stubby leaf-a-life buds. She looked disgruntled.

"Use the banana string to tie up the leaf-a-life to make a circle like a crown," I instructed. I dropped the banana strings I had peeled from the bark of the banana tree earlier, into her lap.

Muncie slinked behind the bedroom door and pulled off her ganzie shirt. I threw her the white sheet I took from Mama's visitor chifforobe.

"This is stupid," Janet muttered loud enough for me to hear. I didn't pay her any mind. All my attention was on Muncie who was tall and would make a good Caesar. I grabbed the sheet from her hands and wrapped her in it, twice around her waist, tight across her flat chest—off the shoulder style— with one brown shoulder exposed. The rest of the sheet I tossed over her shoulder to drape elegantly to the floor. She wiggled her feet into my pair of small rubber thong slippers.

"Is the crown ready?" I asked Janet.

My own toga kept slipping from my other shoulder and threatened to unravel as I placed the crown on Muncie's head. "Now we're ready," I said in glee. "I'll be Brutus, Muncie you're Julius Caesar, step up on this box to give your speech to the senate." I shoved the book in her hand to recite from.

"So who am I?" asked Janet.

"Juuud...Judy where are you? The girls have to go now." My mother's voice echoed through the window.

"Make haste!" I said to my friends. We crumpled the sheets and tossed them under the bed. The girls put on their blouses fast. "Come back tomorrow and we'll finish you hear?" I didn't think they would because they glanced sideways at each other as if they were glad to escape.

All during dinner I plotted the next scene of our play in my head in case my friends returned. I would make Janet the soothsayer bringing the Ides of March. She'd switch roles after Caesar's death and become Marc Anthony to say, "Friends, Romans, Countrymen…"

My mother poised her fork in front of her mouth waiting for me to get back to earth on something she said. Apparently, she mentioned that it was my turn to sleep at my Aunt's house that night. My father shook his head in disgust.

"I tell you Dorcas, this gal pickney is as light as a bottle cork. If you throw her into that water tank outside she'd float."

My brother Donny stifled a laugh behind his fist. He rocked back in his chair, his arms flapping out from his body as if he waded through water. When my parents glanced at him, he pulled in his chair and pretended to scratch the back of his neck. I had no idea what they talked about. At the risk of appearing even dumber, I kept silent, chewing my food.

Donny and I would alternate sleeping out-a-yard with Aunt B because she was lonely after Na-Na died, or she was afraid of duppy. At dusk, before it got dark, I'd take the path to out-a-yard. My steps would quicken when I pass the graveyard as shadows loomed from the banana and pear trees. The last remaining shards of sunlight would dance through the coffee limbs and the branches always dipped to brush against my neck and shoulder.

Aunt B would be waiting for me. She sat on the back stoop with a plate in her hand, chewing and crunching the charred meat which she softened with coconut oil to form curds in the plate.

Aunt B was not a lively conversationalist like Na-Na but she'd listen, giving ho-hum answers. I didn't care because we were of like mind. She was afraid of duppies as much as I was. She disliked harsh rules and would do things that my mother and father didn't like—like cooking when she wanted to even if it was at night, cleaning when she wanted to rather than at a set time. We really became bosom buddies when she said she didn't like the Anglican Church or "Bun Jaw's" milquetoast preaching.

One pitch black night I arrived at Aunt B's house and she announced: "We're going to prayer meeting tonight."

"Is it going to be same like the last?"

"No. Some revival people from Watt Town coming tonight."

I looked forward to these once per month travails, especially since it was a delicious secret from my mother. I wrapped Na-Na's oversized shawl around my shoulders and put on a woolen, floppy hat. Aunt B dressed in a sweater and tie-head.

She carried a bottle lamp—an old aerated water bottle, filled with kerosene oil, the mouth stuffed with scrunched brown paper. It lit our way as we trudged through a forest of trees; huge breadfruit, guinep and star-apple trees dwarfed orange and coffee trees while corn stalks, like flailing arms, leaped at me in the dark.

Peenies, flashing green and bright orange lights, circled us as if they were aliens trying to communicate with silent, shadowy earthlings. I glanced up for a moon but trees formed a canopy overhead. Crickets chirped near and far. Mongoose rustled through the tanzie underbrush while macka hiked up my dress, scratching my bare thighs. I almost fainted when my foot squished down on a bullfrog's mushy back and it croaked.

Aunt B and I huddled close, walking in step like soldiers, my hand shoved high up under her armpit. I stretched my other hand out to push away a branch, my hand disappeared into blackness. I grabbed on to Aunt B's arm with both hands. At last we reached a clearing and millions of twinkling stars burst from the heavens. Perched high in the sky, a little sliver of moon brightened the narrow dirt path.

After we climbed the hill, we stumbled on a building. If not for the huge whitewashed wooden cross in front, I'd bypass it for a church. It had no walls on one side. The other two sides had exposed cement blocks. Rusted steel posts poked from the middle of these blocks, to stand lonely in the moonlight. Only the front entrance wall had a layer of cement with a thin coat of whitewash. Someone had made deep grooves, forming the words "Mt Zion Church," in the cement while it was wet.

We stepped inside the church. A white runner lay across a wooden table with a yellow-gold cross at its center. Inside a glass bowl, bright yellow flowers circled red ones. Anchoring the left side of the table stood a chipped, white enamel basin filled halfway with clear water. A worn bible, a sankey and various pamphlets strewn across the tablecloth, in no particular order, completed the table's decoration.

We eased in the back to sit on narrow wooden planks for benches. No one paid us much attention except for the lazy turning of heads that usually acknowledged a new presence.

About sixty people sat, not dressed formally with lace mantillas on their heads, or elaborate hats, like on Sundays at St. Matthew's Anglican Church. But they came clean and tidy. Women wore little hats or tie-heads, some younger ones had pink and green plastic-covered hair rollers peeking from under cotton head scarves. I tingled with anticipation because Mama and Papa talked about Mt. Zion as a place for the "old hypocrite dem."

My head twisted to the side entrance as the clash of cymbals and crashing tambourines announced the entrance of a dozen women dressed in white. They emerged in single file, dipping their shoulders down and up in a loping dance. They wrapped their heads in white scarves, creating a big knot at their foreheads.

"Ahem, Ahem," the women chanted, leaning forward and back, picking up speed with double steps, to the beat of tambourines. Excitement coursed through me. One after the other they raised their right arms in the air in front, and dropped them as if suddenly heavy. Their faces carried the weight of great sorrow.

The preacher, a little man, wore a long black jacket that reached his knees and the sleeves almost covered his fingers. He was doing a kind of jig. It became clear that this was not our Anglican church and the preacher was not Bun Jaw—our white minister with a permanent sunburn on his cheeks. He drove up from the Parish church every third Sunday.

Miss Miriam sat in the front. Every Friday night, her son Eustace would get drunk and carry on down at the rum bar and the police would drive up in their Landrovers and lock him up.

All the women looked to Miss Miriam to lead. She had a high voice that stood out among everyone else. The sounds of the police sirens signaled that they had taken her beloved Eustace.

Paper fans whirred to get rid of mosquitoes and stirred the sultry air. At this point, Miss Miriam would first begin to wail. I looked expectantly at Aunt B who said in a low voice, "She's just tuning up her pipes." Sure enough, when Miss Miriam found the right note she suddenly burst into song, "Dis lil heart of mine, I'm gonna let it shine, let it shine, let it shine..." Her voice rose to a crescendo while the rest of the congregation backed her in chorus.

Finally a lull, and right on cue, the preacher picked up the bible from the table and waved it in the air proclaiming: "He was a mark for many archers, and they emptied their quivers in him."

"That they did. Lawd they did," Miss Miriam interrupted.

"He was sore, wounded by their calumnies," continued the preacher.

"Amen," the congregation chorused.

"But, he shook..."

"Yes Lawd, Jesus shook dem off..." The congregation rocked from side-to-side on the benches.

"The Lord shook off the venomous beasts..." The preacher held both hands in the air, his body convulsing as if a dog had latched on to his rear end.

By this time, Miss Miriam's face gleamed with a glow, emanating from the depths of her soul. A spasm started in her shoulder and continued in rhythmic jerks throughout every limb of her body. Her breasts rose and fell. Her breathing became shallow. The "Amens" and handclapping rose to a feverish frenzy. Both her feet left the ground and she collapsed in the waiting arms of Granny Lou and the other women. As she crumpled, the dark irises of her eyes disappeared. White foam trickled from one corner of her mouth matching the blank, white eyes, rolling—rolling back in her head.

Miss Gertrude sang plaintively, "tru de night, tru de storm, take my hand precious Lord, for I'm tired…" She had five children. Her husband went off to farm work and she hadn't heard from him since.

While the women rested, they energetically fanned themselves. Aunt B leaned into me with her fan and whispered: "Stop tapping your feet so loud gal before I take off your shoes and slap you on your behind."

Ahem, Ahem, the loping dance started again. This time their faces were a bit more alive. Sweat gave a luminous sheen to their moon-like foreheads. "Meet me by the river, Oh when my Lord shall call me home…" In unison, the women's arms jerked up above their heads then pulled down invisible ropes to their shoulders, their backs crouched and their heads down in supplication. One woman in the back of the line, spun around in a circle then suddenly turned, counterclockwise, her arms making spasmic grasps into the air. Unholy sounds came from her lips, like another language altogether, without any pause.

I pulled on Aunt B's sleeve. "What is she saying?" I asked, hiding my mouth behind the prayer book. I then sat on my hands to quell the trembling.

"The Holy Ghost is in her—quiet!"

I tugged on her blouse again.

"She's speaking in tongues and if you're not quiet you'll soon start too."

I rocked the wooden bench as I sat back, my eyes fixed on the woman. Her mouth was open; her eyes white and blank. My fingers dug into Aunt B's arm but she didn't even flinch. The woman was falling in slow motion. I jumped up from the bench just in time to see the other women grab her just before her head hit the concrete floor. She writhed. I couldn't see her face anymore as a group of people surrounded her. Everyone craned their necks to see.

The preacher called out: "come ye who are heavily laden and I'll give you rest...give your heart to the Lord tonight..." his voice dropped to a whisper... "you may not see tomorrow...come." A line formed in the aisle as people bowed their heads and shuffled up to the altar. The women still sang...a chant now, "lead me home precious Lord."

Tears flowed unchecked down my cheeks.

"Come..." the voice beckoned.

My feet moved and before I knew it, I floated up the aisle with the others. I forgot Aunt B, and everyone else became a blur. My eyes fixed on the preacher mouthing the words, "Come..." drawing me closer and closer.

The preacher laid his hand on my head and sanctification coursed through my body. I was cleansed. Newborn. Pure.

After the service, Aunt B and I walked home

through the shortcut alone. The others went in different directions. I held on to the back of Aunt B's elbow as we walked.

We didn't talk at all. I turned over in my mind that it was indeed a great God that allowed himself to be the target for archers, so he could save us all. I was determined to be worthy of that great sacrifice. I felt drained and wanted to climb in my bed.

I returned to Mt Zion with Aunt B every week, and every week the hypnotic words drew me to repent of sins I didn't know I had. To Aunt B, my being saved never happened. She never spoke of it. One day I ventured to ask why she hadn't gone up to get saved. She said, "Me saved long time."

"So how come I have to go up there every night?" I asked.

"It's the Lord telling you to because you too bloody bad."

For the next week I went around my day-to-day activities pious-like, turning the other cheek to my brother, and to Herby who I'd get in fights with at school. Honor thy mother and father even when I felt the slightest twinge of resentment for any injustice. By the end of the week I was at boiling point. Suddenly, I decided the Anglican Church was easier.

"Aunt B, I don't want to go back to Mt. Zion."

"Choops," she hissed her teeth at me, her wrists deep in soapy suds. She continued to wash the chimmy.

Vexed now, I folded my arms across my chest and pondered that I actually had fun at the Anglican Church. When the choir and the congregation stood for the hymn, "At the cross, at the cross where I first saw the light…" Donny and I would sing at the top of our lungs, "At the cross at the cross where I saw Matty Rass and we'd giggle behind the hymnal and look over to see if Miss Matty or anybody heard us.

"Rass" was the 'bad' word no decent person used.

"It's rass hot;" annoyance at the heat.

"Oh rass;" to shock.

"Kiss me rass;" to surprise.

"I'm going to buss up your rass mouth;" to pick a fight.

He lived in a rass house;" to indicate size.

So mostly the word was used for swearing. And we didn't like Miss Matty.

At our church, Donny and I would get there early every Sunday. He'd play preacher, standing at the pulpit looking important while I was the congregation nodding at him in affirmation when he shook his fist to make a point.

During Bun Jaw's sermon, I could also perch my pink bowl hat at an angle on my head so my parents couldn't see that I slept. Donny would poke me with his elbow when it was time to stand and recite the catechism.

I would start out reciting the first two lines, "I believe in God, the Father Almighty, creator of heaven and earth…" then mumbled the rest.

And I could get away with it all at the Anglican Church without God forcing me down that aisle to confess that I stole Aunt B's coconut drops, even though I always blamed the puss.

My mind was made up. I was not going back to Mt. Zion. But how could I get Aunt B to stop going? I decided to let the cat out of the bag and tell on Aunt B.

I waited until dusk.

"Mama, I don't want to sleep out-a-yard tonight."

"Just go, you know Aunt B's afraid of her shadow and needs your company."

"But I—."

"You hear me pickney! Get ready and go before it gets dark."

Crickets had already started their nattering through the coffee trees. And I had to pass the tombs. No help for it. I had to get on with it.

"I don't want to go to Mt. Zion again." I blurted out, a mulish expression on my face.

"Say what?"

"Mt Zion."

It was now or never. I had to let her understand. "The hypocrite place you and Papa talked about over dinner," I said on a rush almost tripping over my tongue.

"You mustn't listen to big people's discussions that don't concern you." She gave me a cutting glare then flayed the dish towel in the air. The same way she flayed the belt before a whipping. I trembled involuntarily but she started to dry the dishes instead. "You mean to tell me Aunt B took you to Mt. Zion?"

"Yes mam." My mouth felt parched.

"Hmm." She dried her hand in the dish towel then on her skirt. "Wait right here don't move."

Her face set, she strode with deliberate steps past the kitchen room, under the clothesline and I knew she was going to the verandah where my father perched every evening. He'd have his felt hat on his head and he'd greet passersby as they went about their evening pursuits. I sat on the stoop and waited—counting ants.

A few minutes later my father's white hair bobbed up and down across from the high water tank. Then in his easy, nonchalant way he strolled on the path to out-a-yard. When he passed the tombs I heard his loud trademark sigh, expelling everything he had pent up for the day in one long breath. I felt a twinge of regret and sorry for Aunt B. She didn't stand a chance between those two—my father's studied calmness and my mother's fiery instigation. I felt like Brutus who betrayed Julius Caesar.

"Go and read your book until your father get back," my mother said, before she followed my father at a distance to eavesdrop.

I went inside my bedroom; laid across the bed and rummaged through the huge carton of books

I called my treasure chest. These books were way beyond my age level that my sister's husband stored with us before he left for America. I didn't feel worthy enough to read Na-Na's bible so   I read Julius Caesar. I'd know the sections by heart when my friends returned. From my first reading when I was six, two years before, I never really understood what Caesar meant when he said *"Et tu, Brute,"* right before he was stabbed to death. I understood it better now. I reread and recited the lines where Brutus told the Senate that he loved Caesar but loved Rome and freedom more.

Later, my parents talked in low tones on the verandah. My father's unruffled tone soothed my mother's agitated one. Then he lapsed into silence leaving only my mother's voice. As usual, the silence won. Soon after, my mother entered my room. She looked angry. "Get your nightie. You're going to sleep with Aunt B."

"But it's dark…midnight," I said in alarm. My eyes shot through the window, I couldn't even make out the jackfruit tree. My eyes darted back to her. "Who's going to take me?"

"You too lie again. She said, chuckling. "It's just past dusk-dusk. You don't need anyone to take you—just go!"

She flounced out to the verandah. I sat on the edge of my bed stunned. I had to face the dark. I heard them both chuckling on the verandah. I clutched Julius Caesar in my hands and leaped out of bed to pound on my brother's door but he didn't answer. I called out to Mordecai, my father's help, who slept in the kitchen room, no answer. I went to Jen's room. She was singing and hemming her dress again. "Jen please, can you walk with me to Aunt B?"

"How much you're going to pay me?"

"I can give you one of my books."

"Who want your stupid book? Just go on, I don't have time right now."

She went back to her humming. I went back to my room and threw Julius Caesar back in the box and picked up my nightgown. I wasn't going to beg anyone to accompany me. I could do this.

With new resolve, I boldly stepped on to the path with my heart in my mouth. I slowed my footsteps when I saw the endless blackness ahead. Filled with trepidation, I ducked under the low orange tree branch. Coffee branches grazed my arms but I mumbled, "I know you're just coffee trees, nothing else." Every organ inside my body trembled. I whispered over and over, "coffee trees, orange trees…that's all…"

On the right I passed the white-washed tombs in stark contrast to the black night. Goosebumps dotted my arms one-by-one. My voice faltered when a breeze or mongoose rustled the coffee trees to my left.

I didn't look.

The back of my head tingled and began to grow. I hugged my nightie under my armpit in a death grip; my fingers punched holes through the lace neckline. With elbows locked to my waist, my shoulders hunched, I listened.

Even the crickets had stopped chirping as if waiting for something to happen.

Talking to the trees wasn't cutting it anymore. I needed something stronger. On a gust of inspiration and much bravado, I bellowed a hymn I learned at the Anglican Church.

"Guide me, O though Great Jehovah, pilgrim through this barren land; I am weak, but thou art mighty; hold me with thy powerful hand…"

I picked up speed, half-walking and half-running. I wanted to sing again but was afraid of hearing my own voice stretching in the vast silence.

I panted a tuneless, "Guide me…guide me…" I cleared my throat and started again. "Jehovah… guide me…O though great Jehovah…." I had passed the tombs. I gave a quick glance over my shoulder to see if any white thing followed me.

But the hard part was yet to come.

I had to go up a slope and the dirt path turned at the star-apple tree. I didn't know what lurked around the corner. My fingers had now worked their way clear through the lace neckline of my nightgown to form lace rings on every finger. I couldn't even breathe now, much less sing, but my lips managed to mouth the words: "Though I walk through the valley of the shadow of death I'll fear no evil ... for thou art my rod and staff..."

Out of the corner of my eyes the stately banana trees lined the path, their umbrella leaves touching. I pretended the banana trees were my private army sent to protect me as I stalked through this valley of death with my head held high. When I stubbed my toe on a bump in the path near to the guinep tree, I knew I was almost there. I broke into a full run, my nightie now slung over my right shoulder. I stubbed my toe again by the latrine, and almost leaped in delight when Aunt B's dog "Delicate" started yapping but came to greet me.

I ran fast to the house, jumped the three steps to the back door, and pounded on it with all my might.

"Aunt, Aunt, let me in, let me in!"

The bottom latch pulled back with a click and she ratched back the rusted top latch with a resounding thud. I was never so glad to see a human being. I pitched headlong into the hall.

"Who and you come out?" Aunt B asked.

"Just me," I said and plopped down in the armchair by the window feeling drained and thankful. I breathed in the scent of Bay Rum in the dim room lit by one big lamp in the corner.

"Outside... Delicate... Out!" Aunt B shouted as she closed the door on the dog. But Delicate nudged it open with his butt and skittered under the dining table.

"This damn dog know him have no place inside," she grumbled. "Where is the broom?"

She reached for the broom handle that leaned against the door hinges then bent low and tried to sweep him out.

Delicate wouldn't budge.

He squealed in a piteous tone. The door was still open. I wished Aunt B would hurry and close it. What if something followed me inside? Maybe that was why Delicate didn't want to stay outside. I decided to plead on his behalf.

"He's just under the table. He's not doing anything."

"What do you think I have him for, to swaddle in the house like baby? He's a watchdog; he needs to be outside to let me know who's coming."

Much good he was going to do as a watchdog. Delicate limped on three legs; he couldn't set the left hind leg on the ground. From where I sat I could see him curled up in the corner under the table, looking frightened.

The door was still open and the air had turned decidedly chilly in the room. I decided to help. I cornered him at one end and Aunt B shoved him with the broom along the linoleum floor. Delicate skidded on his backside, his legs up in the air. At last he was out and she slammed the door. I felt sorry for Delicate but at least the door was closed.

Aunt B rested the broom back against the crack in the door. I followed her into the bedroom, her long flannel nightgown swirling around her small frame. She had her hair done up for the night in "chiney bumps" and a cotton scarf, sapped in Bay Rum, tied across her forehead. The lamp wick was already turned down and it emitted a spark of light like one lonely star in the sky. The flame flickered, casting elongated shadows on the wall. "Vup...vup...vup," were the only sounds that filled the room as the lamp's wick sucked oil from its round glass base. It would only be another 30 minutes or so before the final "vup" and the room would plunge into darkness. Now was the time Aunt B would confront me about my actions.

I removed my skirt and hung it on the protruding nail behind the door; then my blouse. I put on the ripped nightgown and hopped over to the corner of the bed against the wall. I waited for her to begin the conversation.

Aunt B sat on the edge of the bed, her chin resting in her palm.

"You mean to tell me that your mother and father send you out here all by yourself?"

"Yes," I answered, wondering when she was going to get to the part about me telling on her about Mt. Zion. I clutched the blanket to my chin and didn't volunteer anything else.

"Bwoy, bwoy they are hard people..."

I didn't answer. I couldn't think of anything to say. She stretched out next to me.

Silence, except for the fast "vup, vup, vup" sounds coming from the lamp.

"Ju, I forgot to ask you," she said. My heart plummeted. Now she was getting to it. "Did you want some Milo to drink before you go to bed?"

I did but I said no. "Are we going back to Mt. Zion?" I blurted.

"No," she said. "You want your puppa kill me?"

I laid there for a while going over in my mind the many ways I could say I was sorry that I told on her. Finally I got it.

"Aunt…" I whispered.

Silence. Steady breathing. A long tremulous sigh escaped, short snagging snores rose from the pit of her belly.

Guilt seeped over me as I watched the shadows dance on the opposite wall. I could make out one tall shadowy shape with a reed for a crown on his head. Julius Caesar, I thought, through sleep-laden eyes. Just before I fell into sleep's oblivion, another shadow lurked then leaped behind Caesar.

Et tu Brute? I thought.

Vup!

Thawing Out in Bamboo Grove Village

Going home...
What you pack doesn't matter...
just the basics
What you need
A little bit here, a little bit there...
of nothing.
How do you pack up a life?
You don't.
You leave it behind to gather dust.
From dust it came and dust it returns.
Here's what to pack...
Your heart
Wrap twice in cellophane
Place in a ziplock bag
Don't check it in your suitcase
Take it in your carry-on
When you arrive at your destination
Place it in the freezer for a while
And wait until it's time to thaw.

All In The Cards

"My green card is missing."

Judy's voice came from a distance, like the sound of a coconut shell with its inside flesh hollowed. Her French-manicured fingers scooped the remains of her handbag on to the car seat. She looked in her brass-gilded powder compact just to make sure the card wasn't in there. During this time she felt the immigration official's steely grays assessing her.

Judy forced a smile. "I must have misplaced the card somewhere."

He gazed at her unblinking. She shrugged.

"It's not like I committed a crime or anything."

Silence.

Tiny beads of perspiration sprinkled her nose and upper lip. Her armpits felt warm and slimy. "I do have other identification," she said, attempting a last ditch winning smile.

He picked up the phone. Instinctively she glanced over her shoulder as if seeking help from somewhere. But only the Maple Leaf flag waved forlornly in the evening breeze basking over Lake Erie. She shifted in her seat. The Star Spangled Banner across the border stood erect; not one bit affected by the breeze. He murmured in the phone.

A tiny smile tugged at one corner of his mouth and he said: "Pull over to the side ma'am." He stopped the cars in the other lines so she could get by. All eyes focused on Judy—some curious, some questioning, some condemning. A few had the "gotcha" look.

"My God," she seethed. "You would think I was pushing dope or something."

Two officers met her. They opened her car door and marched her toward a one-story building. She couldn't help noticing the black Volkswagen, the door open, one leg of a blue uniform jutting in the air. The officer was prying the inside lining of the car. On the terrace, she side-stepped an opened suitcase, its contents in disarray with the owner's eyes downcast, lips pursed.

A woman was escorted to a nearby office, her burgundy headscarf disappearing through the doorway. The woman's husband followed, his crisp white tunic billowing over loose-fitting pants. Over to the north corner, a child cuddled her ethnic Barbie while her mother talked earnestly to an officer. The little girl's small round eyes shone bright like the colored beads dangling from the ends of her Nubian braids.

Judy continued to walk, a step behind the official, down a long corridor. Her heels made clickety-clack noises on the slate blue vinyl tiles. She blinked as they ushered her into a tiny room flooded with harsh, fluorescent lighting. A petite woman with a split-ended pony tail sat at the rectangular, folding table. Judy perched on the low wooden bench in front of the woman and waited. The woman added a fresh stick of gum to the old one in her mouth and thumbed through a manila folder with forms. Without bothering to look up, she said, "name?"

"Judy Alethia Gordon."

"Nationality?"

"Jamaican."

"Where do you live?"

"41 Elm Street, North Hempstead, Long Island, New York.

"Why were you in Canada?"

"Visiting family."

"Do you have a job in the States?"

"Yes. I work as a legal secretary with Myers, Coombs & Silverstein, Park Avenue, New York City."

"Place your pocket book on the table."

Judy handed over the bag. The official rummaged through the contents and removed her wallet. She took out all of the cards, Blue Cross, Costco, Lord & Taylor, Amoco, American Express and more—spreading them in a semi-circle as if playing the tarots. She hunched over the cards, examining each one. Finally, she pulled one from the semi-circle—a thin, onion skin, shriveled square. She held it in front of the fluorescent lamp.

"Uh-oh," Judy said under her breath. The Death Card.

The official looked at her for the first time, taking in the impeccably layered hairdo, the expressive almond eyes and toffee-glossed lips in one sweeping glance. Raising one eyebrow she asked, "What is this?"

"My driver's license," Judy said. "It's been through the washer and dryer…twice," she finished in a tremulous, small voice.

The officer smirked. "Been making a lot of mistakes lately haven't you, Miss Gordon? First your green card disappeared, now your license's messed up. So technically you have no valid identification."

Judy's heart sank.

"You also have nice friends. They allowed you to put over 600 miles on their car?"

"Y-y-yes, my cousin and her husband have three cars and they loaned me one for the weekend."

A new official entered the room to join the interrogation. His alert eyes scanned the folder.

His hooked nose gave him a distinct, hawk-like appearance. He peered at Judy. "So…your prospective employer loaned you their car?"

Judy blinked rapidly in confusion.

Without waiting for a response, the hawk continued. "I understand Long Island is a wealthy suburb and they employ women from the islands to care for their homes and children, don't they Miss Gordon?"

"I have no idea what you're talking about."

But she knew. She had witnessed the lawyers she worked for try to befuddle witnesses on the stand. Anger began to warm the tip of her toes, up through her body, like the hot, ginger-root tea her mother used to give her when she felt sick.

"Sure you don't," the woman drawled in a honeyed tone. "For your friends left the car in Toronto, so you could sneak across the border. Isn't that so Miss Gordon?"

The silk scarf, tied loosely at Judy's nape suddenly became a noose.

"No you are so wrong. It's not like that at all."

Her size eight denim pants suit felt as if they had shrunken to a size four. Tears welled up and ran freely down her cheeks. The hawk glanced at the woman and they both shrugged. He left the room.

"If you will only listen," Judy pleaded, her palms clasped tightly under her chin. "I do have my green card but…"

"Well," the woman said, clicking her chewing gum and rocking back in her chair. "Since you claim that you have a green card, what does it look like?"

Judy's throat constricted. She could swear she had just grown an Adam's apple. She swallowed hard. Her nostrils flared. She stared fixedly beyond the woman's head at a spot on the wall. The spot seemed to grow and blur into myriad images of former slaves carrying their 'free passes' at all times. Always having to give an account. Where they are from. Where they are going. Never truly free. Dammit, this was the 80's! Her anger exploded, erasing rational thought. She slammed her fist down on the table. "It's just a goddam piece of paper, that's what it is!"

The official looked at her with a level gaze then she raised her haunches inch-by-inch from the chair leaning across the table toward Judy. Eye to eye, nose to nose, her 'Juicy Fruit' breath fanning Judy's face. The woman's thin lips curled. Spiky hair protruded slightly from her nostrils and a feathery, blond moustache caressed the top of her vertically lined, chapped lips.

"Just a little piece of paper, huh?" She smiled an unworldly smile. "Is that what you call this privilege? Gimme your wrists!"

Judy couldn't help musing that the woman's movements had suddenly become quick and purposeful, as if fired by a new resolve: "For the good of country...for America!" Reality hit Judy hard when she felt the cold metal handcuffs clamp her wrist. Her legs buckled with the enormity of her situation.

"O'Brien, are you ready?"

The hawk and another official stood at the door, jingling keys.

"In just a minute," the woman replied. She turned to answer Judy's questioning look. "Until you can produce your green card you'll be detained."

"You mean in a jail?"

"If you want to call it that."

"Can I please call my family?"

"Be my guest," she said, almost graciously beckoning her to a pay phone. She had to call collect. She dialed her sister's number in Toronto. No answer. She called her brother in Brampton. The phone rang. Judy held it tight. While it rang she glanced out the window. All she could see was the fading violet of an evening sky. Shadowy blobs of purple lurked over the horizon. Judy counted twenty five rings until the operator's recorded voice jolted her: The person whom you are trying to reach is not available at this time. Please try your call again." She hung up the phone and turned to her jailers in defeat.

"Of course, no one is home," the woman said, glancing impishly at the two men. "You can try again later, but first we have to send you back."

"Back where?"

Alarm rushed through her like a lightning bolt,

making her eyes pop. They were going to deport her! She imagined returning to the island in disgrace.

"The Canadian officials will have to decide what to do with you—they are the ones who let you in."

Oh my God—a reprieve! She had an idea where to find the confounded green card. It was still in her apartment in New York.

They marched her over to the Canadian side and handed her to the Canadian immigration. The new officials seemed more civil even when they told her she would be detained at their facility in Hamilton. Judy knew from her frequent visits to Toronto that Hamilton was only an hour away. The new officials filled out more forms, asking the same questions and getting the same answers until she wondered if she was in the movie, Groundhog Day.

The sky turned a deep purple blanket. No tinge of violet remained as Judy rode with two officials in the backseat of a Dodge Aries K, its side and back windows heavily grilled. She listened to their conversation, sprinkled with "heavy rains ...GST tax...hydro bills...drinking pop," until she fell into an exhausted doze.

Judy awakened as the car idled up to an imposing building and skidded in the mud.

"Careful, don't step out into the mud. We don't want it tracking inside and messing up the floors."

With her head down, she picked her way across the parking lot between the two officials. The air was thin and cool, the soft ground gave slightly beneath her feet.

Inside the sterile looking reception area, a heavy-set woman waited. She studied the file and fidgeted with the narrow belt encircling her high middle. Her cherubic face belied her formidable figure. Finally she said, "Come on and get undressed."

She beckoned for Judy to follow her into the narrow dressing room.

"Undressed?" Judy's mouth formed an 'O.'

"Yep, take it all off—underwear, bra, everything."

Judy glanced at her in consternation. She wondered if the woman was going to leave and give her some privacy. The woman only wiggled her upper torso to keep the belt from sliding up under her breasts.

"Now spread your legs open. Bend and touch your toes."

Good God, no, not Miss Dorcas' fine daughter being treated like this. Judy began to sob. Tears washed her face, mascara burned her eyes. Sooty tears formed rivulets, streaming down her naked breasts.

"Put this on and c'mon back," the woman said, twirling a pair of silver handcuffs in the air as she strode out the door. Judy looked in disdain at the peach, seersucker smock. The last time she wore anything remotely like this was back in Bamboo Grove. She had helped her momma bake totoes, bulla cakes and coconut drops for the harvest supper at Mt. Zion church. Every now and then a treat would accidentally fall into the large pocket of the smock. Momma never missed a trick. She would squeeze her lips together, to a sharp point, rocking back and forth on her heels, eye-balling her. Judy's eyes misted with fresh tears for those good old days.

Why had she come here? She asked herself as she tied the strings down the side of her smock. Like everyone else... seeking economic prosperity. She squelched the thought that she had really wanted to escape the confines of an island and be free to spread her wings. How ironic that her freedom was now an issue in the proverbial "land of the free." Judy could see the cards were now stacked high against her. She was in a simmering pot of red stew peas, and she was one of the peas, being busted from all sides.

Between muffled sobs, hiccups and sniffles, the voice of her momma travelled thousands of miles across shimmering waves of aquamarine, echoing off tree-covered mountain peaks: Stop sitting there like a lump 'o lard, feeling all sorry. Shake up yourself chile and 'play the hand you got!'

Like adding super octane to her fifteen-year old Toyota, the charge was palpable. The tears ceased. She came to the realization that alternately firing off at the mouth and sniveling wasn't working. She had to be rational and try to do something about her situation. With as much dignity as she could muster, she strode back into the room, her shoulders squared, chin lifted a notch. She spoke in a clear, resonant voice:

"You know, I was quite overwhelmed and shocked by the allegations. I can assure you that I do possess an Alien Registration Card. You see, in my rush to start the trip, I had left it in New York, along with my passport and some traveler's checks in the inside pocket of my coat. At the last minute, I decided I didn't need the coat, since the weather was getting nice. There must be some way to verify that I'm a landed resident."

"Did you tell the U.S. officials that?"

"Well, not exactly…"

"They must have reason to believe that you are an alien. It's your responsibility to prove it," the woman said with a hint of sympathy in her tone.

"So what's going to happen now?"

"We-l-l," she said drawing out the word. If you can't prove you are a resident, you'll be deported."

Judy's new found strength dissipated. What if the card was not where she thought it was. What if it had fallen out at the rest stop?

The woman pointed to a red phone on top of a bookcase. "You may want to call someone?"

Judy jumped at the chance, to yet dreading the unanswered rings. This time Clarence answered on the first ring and she choked up.

"Clarence, Clarence…please help me…please. They threw me in jail…"

"Calm down, will you? What for?"

"Clarence you have to come and get me. I forgot my green card."

"Be cool…you won't be the first nor the last to be in jail for something like this. Let me speak with the official and I'll see what I can do."

"See what you can do? What you can do?" Her voice rose to a hysterical pitch. "Please, please you have to come now…I can't sleep here." She dropped her voice to a whine. "Ibetcockroachesarecrawlingalloveronthebed and…"

"Let me speak with the official," he said in a kindly tone.

Judy handed the phone to the woman, not meeting her eyes. "My brother would like to speak with you."

After the woman gave him details on the bond he needed for Judy's release she hung up and said, "follow me." Judy dried her face on the shoulder of her smock. They walked down a dim hallway with bars on both sides. This was worse than the movie *Groundhog Day*. It was the freaking *Twilight Zone!* Visions of Hitchcock's *Vertigo* also ran through her mind as she swayed unsteadily down the endless corridor. She recoiled from what existed in the dark behind the bars.

The eerie silence unsettled her as eyes watched every step she made; eyes she couldn't see, only feel. The warden stopped abruptly, removing the fat bunch of keys from her narrow belt. She opened the grill and firmly pressed Judy's back, indicating she should enter.

The iron gate slammed shut.

Judy stood in stunned silence, her eyes slowly adjusting to the dark cell. She sidled against the wall, grateful for its solidity. She inched her way towards the silhouette of what must be a bed. The sound of heavy breathing made her pause, flattening her body against the wall.

"Yo betta climb up de ladder to de top bunk," muttered a groggy voice with a territorial edge. Judy proceeded to do just that. If she could lie down, close her eyes and fall into oblivion, morning would come soon. Even with this rational thought, loud guttural sobs escaped her throat. As the night stretched on, the sobs grew in intensity until a direct kick landed in the small of her back, through the thin mattress from the occupant below.

"Mwen pa ka domi!"

The Haitian woman's outburst felt like a slap against the cheek of a hysterical child. Judy instantly calmed, in midst of a hiccup, and soon drifted into sleep. She dreamed she was free-falling down a dark hole without sides—or any bottom.

Morning came with a piercing alarm renting the air. Judy peered down from her high bunk, through the rails. All she could see was the bottom half of a woman with sensible, laced-up black shoes and thick ribbed stockings. The legs paced back and forth, hands balled up in fists behind her butt. "I'm giving you five minutes to get dressed ladies, then into the canteen. Move it!"

Judy scrambled to her feet, jumping past the now empty bed of the territorial voice and joined the line of women. She was starving. Her bladder was also bursting. She gave her tray to the server who handed her two burnt slices of toast and a tepid cup of black tea.

"Dear God, where is Clarence?" she muttered.

What if no one came to get her out? Anxiety gnawed at her and she shoved a slice of toast in her mouth. Women began to assemble for exercises. Judy hurriedly drank the tea, washing down the gritty particles of toast in her mouth. Suddenly her name boomed over the loudspeaker, "GOR-DON, we have no prima donnas in here." She jumped to join the other women.

Drinking the tea was a mistake. Her bladder was ready to pop. She walked in a crouch, contracting pelvic muscles that she didn't realize she had. The warden's voice now louder—"up, one, two, three, four jumping jacks…" Judy found a space in the back row. She wondered: How do you excuse yourself to go to the restroom in jail. Do you put your hands up like in grade school? She would not dare interrupt. She instead simulated the movements of the other women. Heels together, knees bent outward, her body bobbing straight up and down like ballet plies and demi-plies. What would she do when it came to the jumping jacks?

A woman walked in from the side door, mincing her steps in wedged heel shoes. She wore a hobble skirt, a paisley print blouse, and an expression that said, I'm from the office. She whispered in the warden's ear who motioned to Judy. "Follow her, Gordon."

Clarence must be here, Judy thought with elation. She held her head low, eyes refusing to meet the stares of the other inmates. Wanting to follow the warden's exact instructions she walked behind Miss Mincy Steps all the way.

"Excuse me ma'am, I would like to use the bathroom before I go for the interview."

The woman paused in stride and pointed straight ahead. "I'll wait outside and escort you to the office."

"Uh-ok, thanks." Judy's spirits drooped a little. She was still a prisoner.

Judy hugged her personal belongings and headed to the bathroom. It was like entering an inner sanctorum. Private. She peed for a long time. As long as that day when the Grade 4 teacher, Ms. Garvey, had strapped her with a belt in front of the class—for not knowing the percentage of some number. She had felt the gush, then the hot trickles down to her inside ankle, filling her loafers. In a silent plea, Judy had placed her leg against Ms. Garvey's. The woman's eyes dilated with dawning horror as the warmth penetrated her stockings.

The prison clock chimed noon. Judy felt drained. She leaned against the cold, steel paneling and composed herself. Dressing unhurriedly, she savored the feel of her silk knee-highs gliding over her calves. Two women entered the bathroom. Judy peeked through the gap at the door hinge, trying to see their faces. She wondered if they could also see her. Their wet clothing and umbrellas left tiny pools of water on the concrete floor. Alternately blowing and sniveling up their noses, they talked in a nasal pitch about the depressing rain and disgusting mud outside. The voices trailed away and Judy ventured from the stall and out in the hallway where Miss Mincy Steps waited. She motioned for Judy to follow her down a corridor, to the room for her interview with the immigration official.

Judy sat on the bench for an hour, mostly staring at the rain trickling down the window pane and flattening out into an ugly smear. Finally, a bald-headed man with a cherub face emerged from the room with Clarence towering over him.

Clarence's face looked drawn. His lips tight over his teeth as if he had root canal and the Novocain hadn't worn off. The man was saying: "Don't forget, she is in your charge for the next five days." He held up five fingers, as if Clarence couldn't count. "You'll be held accountable, and your bond confiscated if she does not...I repeat...does not...report to this office with her proper documents by Monday."

"Are you sure that's all she'll need, sir?" Clarence asked in a mock English accent.

"Everything we need to release her is in the card, Mr. Gordon."

He proceeded to count off the five fingers:

"(1) her alien number; (2) her fingerprint; (3) date of entry; (4) signature, and; (5) all the other codes that we recognize."

Clarence nodded his head to show understanding. All the time his eyes searched Judy's, transmitting the message: I hope you know where your card is. She gave him an over-bright grin and a thumbs-up. His face visibly relaxed.

By the time Clarence and Judy stepped outside, the rain had turned into a steady drizzle. The sky took on the cast of tarnished silver. Mud splattered the pavement like cinnamon sprinkled bread pudding. It was the kind of mud that would stick to car tires, forming crusty lumps on fenders. Judy spread five fingers in front of her brother's face then bubbled with laughter. He joined in, giving her a big embrace. They dashed to the car, hop scotching over puddles. Behind them, with each drop of rain, the soft mud oozed and quietly obliterated their footprints.

Easy Riders

They ride in alone or in a pack...
        dressed in gray, charcoal or pitch black.
One glides in through vaporized air with disdain
        like a toothy witch on a spindly broom,
        sinking her fangs in flesh, suffer the pain!
Sometimes they ride in on their Harleys ... vroom!
        changing gears by your ears, then they bite,
        sucking your juices to their sweet delight.
And before you can swat the infinitesimal gnats
        they'll zoom off into the night like vampiry bats.

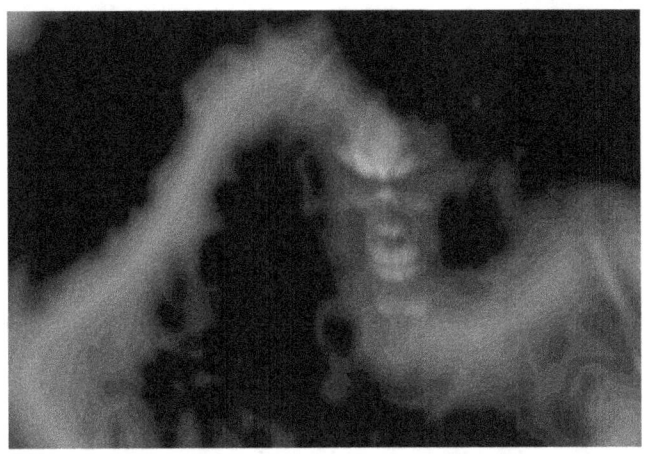

Doo's Duppy

When I turned 13, I left Bamboo Grove and moved in with Auntie Elaine, her husband Linford, and their baby Doo at Mr. Gunter's house. I no longer had to commute from my village to attend high school.

Mr. Gunter was a very fair-skinned man with straight, slicked hair. He drove a light blue Austin Cambridge car with the back almost hitting the ground and the front hiked in the air. He and Mrs. Gunter would sit in the front seats looking as if they were in a rocket ready to blast off into space. Mr. Gunter was our landlord and his house was next to ours. The house we rented was situated in a gully. If you walked on the road and looked down, houses were nestled in a valley-like setting. I always prayed that a rum-sodden driver would not careen off the road and tumble on our roof.

Now this house was a ranch with two bedrooms, a living room, kitchen, a verandah and carport. Big leafy banana trees and various citrus trees surrounded the house. Lying in my bed at night, I could always hear the whirr, whirr of cars with the occasional screeching of tires, and impatient honks and trucks shifting gears as they hauled white marl to the nearby factory. I was always glad I wasn't walking on the sidewalk-less road and having to hop up on the embankment to avoid getting run over.

Now Doo was the first grandson in the family and everyone adored him. He was a cute and happy baby, and a delight to be around.

But one day he changed.

He became sick and listless.

He was taken to numerous doctors, no one could find out what was wrong. One day, while the adults were away, I baby sat. All of a sudden, the baby got animated in my arms. He kept looking over my shoulder and pointing. He then chuckled to himself. I felt the hair at my nape stiffen, a tingling up my spine and my head tightened as if all my brain cells were squishing together. When Doo laughed, I spun around to look behind me. There was nothing.

No one was more relieved than I, when his parents returned home.

The next night, I was awakened at about 4 a.m. from a deep sleep. Someone was walking with deliberate, unhurried footsteps past my door. It was neither Auntie Elaine's light footsteps nor Uncle Linford's mincy walk. I called out.

"Who is that?"

Silence.

I crawled out of bed and tiptoed to the door's entrance. No one was there. I made a big leap into my aunt's room and another leap into their bed.

"What's wrong?" They said, jumping up in unison.

"A duppy!" I said, shaking, and laying in a coil at the foot of their bed.

"Choops. Go back to sleep." I wouldn't budge.

Doo started to wail in his crib and they soon forgot about me in their bed.

They patted him but he squirmed, making a great effort to look behind his father. Uncle Linford finally raised the baby to shoulder level and immediately Doo's eyes roamed as if following someone's movements.

But no one was there.

Finally, Doo slumped in his father's arms. His eyes rolled back until only the whites showed. He stiffened, flexing his arms and legs out straight. Uncle Linford shoved him into his wife's arms and in seconds the car engine revved up in the carport. They were off to the hospital.

Thank goodness it was morning. Still shaking from the visit from Doo's Duppy, I hurriedly left for school. The schoolyard was empty. I was the earliest at school. However, I had a full day before I had to deal with Doo's Duppy again.

Something had to be done. Doctors could not cure Doo and he was getting sicker every day. His illness was a mystery to everyone in the town—especially the market higglers who made it the talk of the day.

"De baby too young to eat solid food. Me hear say when him poo is nothing but callaloo come out."

"You mean de green, green callaloo? But baby no suppose fe nyam callaloo. A what dis pon de po pickney?"

"Smaddy set duppy pon de baby."

"But mi hear say is Mr. Gunter dead mother a play with de pickney and feed de baby callaloo."

"Marse Linford and Miss Elaine will haffi bun de duppy out of de house or else it gwine kill de baby."

"Either bun some croton bush round de house or sprinkle Kananga water in a every room corner."

"Dat dere duppy would bust out a laugh—Kananga water!"

"Dem haffi use de genuine *Wray and Nephew* white rum and dash it so it run and soak in a every corner. A hard duppy dat."

It was official around the town. We were living in

a haunted house. The helper packed up to leave but not before she set two senseh fowls to run around in the backyard.

"Where did these fowls come from?" Auntie Elaine asked in annoyance. She bought all her chickens from Chin's Supermarket and did not take kindly to live ones messing up her yard.

"Nutten run duppy like senseh fowl Miss Elaine. Mi borrow dem from Miss Pauline down de road. She will come for dem tomorrow."

"Rubbish! The duppy is inside the house."

"You don't know, Miss Elaine, smaddy might grudge you fe you pretty baby and plant guzu inna de yard. If smaddy plant it, den de senseh fowl wi diggy up."

After the helper left with her suitcase, Auntie Elaine took a leave of absence from her job at the parish council to care for Doo. The next morning, Saturday, I was still in bed, the house quiet. Auntie had told me the night before that she was leaving with Doo and Uncle Linford early to take care of some business.

I was alone in the house.

All of a sudden a thunderous crash came from the kitchen. Pots and pans were being tossed to the floor while the cupboard doors slammed.

I called out in a weak voice. No answer.

The ruckus in the kitchen continued.

I rose from the bed, my knees shaking, grabbed

my terry robe hanging on a nail behind the door, and darted through the living room to the verandah. I leaned over the rail and yelled for Mr. Gunter.

By the time Mr. Gunter came, the house was quiet like a morgue—and as cold.

"Mr. Gunter sir, the duppy is in the kitchen now. It's mad because the baby gone."

"Nuh tell me foolishness you hear pickney. What duppy?"

"Is true suh!"

"Ooonu too bloody fool-fool. Nutten nuh go so!"

"Can I come and stay on your verandah until my Auntie comes back?"

"What a botheration! Come on then."

While I sat on Mr. Gunter's verandah I made the decision, school or no school, I was going home to Bamboo Grove to my parents. I would not live in a haunted house.

Fortunately, I didn't have to make that decision. Soon after, my family returned with a moving truck. We would not spend another night in that house.

All our friends and neighbors came to help us pack and move. Doo was secluded away in Bamboo Grove with my mother. With the house a bustle of activity, I did not give the duppy a second thought. As our car pulled out of the driveway, I looked back. I wondered if the duppy was watching us go. I shivered and goose bumps ran up my arms. Would the duppy follow us?

Over the next few months, in the new house, we keep careful watch over Doo. No sign of the duppy. Doo is thriving and happy again.

But now, he has a special liking for callaloo.

Farrin Meets Local

Mr. Pinnock hails a route taxi
squeezing in as the fourth man
on the backseat.
Off to Grand Market in High Town.
He's never been to Farrin and doesn't
have any desire to leave what he's known.
He pays his two Sangster bills and slams the taxi
door.
He finds a makeshift bench to sit and munch—
his slice of black cake, wishing for more
but washing it down with a sorrel Sky Juice.
Loud music from two jukeboxes clashes in his ear,
raucous laughter,
boisterous arguing,
women walking this way and that in colorful outfits.
He chuckles at a dimpled butt in neon, skinny pants.
His people.
His eyes fixate on the man walking down the street
with a familiar gait—like he's stepping over hot
coals,
sporting blue, iridescent, dark glasses
silk pants
silk shirt

Jerry curl tendril dangling between his brows

Boasy.

He stops short in front of Mr. Pinnock.

Wait a who dis? The farriner says.

Mr. Pinnock stands, racking his brain wondering…

is it really Chigger Foot Busta who left for farrin eons ago?

"Whassup Dawg?" The man says, raising his arm to high-five.

Mr. Pinnock's smile fades. "Dawg, Dawg? A who you a call dawg?"

"Maaan, 'ow long as it been? Damn good to see you Dawg!"

"Mi name Pinnock! Ah Pinnock a mi name in case you fegat! Wha de Bumbo you a call me dawg fah!"

"Cool it nuh me brethren, a just 'ow we greet each other abroad you know?"

"Ah so? Den you can go right back deh and tun dawg. Me a smaddy yah!"

Ode to the Pumpkin Man

The pumpkin man grows 'em by the dozens
and exports them to foreign lands with the
help of all his cousins.

While the pumpkin's still on the stem
he makes an incision fills it with weed
and causes mayhem!

One slips from the inspector's thumb,
and falls to the ground
making a splatter.

As the onlookers gather,
the inspector makes his decision
to lock up the pumpkin man forever!

Sandcastles

Winnifred was only 18 when she left Jamaica with her new husband Lionel. They made their home with their daughter, Christina, in Brixton, England where they lived for 40 years. She a nurse, he a civil servant.

"Lord Lionel, we going home!"

"Yes Winnie, God is good."

"No more money worries. We have we pension come straight to us in Jamaica. No more hustle and bustle."

"You leave out the most important thing though." He inhaled deeply from his pipe. "No more of this bloody cold!"

"Or the bloody rain and damp!" She did a little jig with her hips.

"Woman, what a way you frisky!"

That was six months ago. Lionel and Winnie are now bastions of the Bamboo Grove community in Jamaica. Winnie isn't a woman to slouch around the house. She gives back to the community that spawned her. She is on the school board, the clinic board, the church board and formed her own women's group with other returnees to beautify Bamboo Grove.

Meanwhile, Lionel, in Winnie's mind, has become an idler. He spends most of his time at the beach, building sandcastles that are so fantastic that they attract tourists and locals alike.

And that's where the trouble begins.

For the first time in their marriage, Winnie feels him drifting away from her. They used to be so connected back in England. She remembers the times when they would snuggle by the fireplace with a glass of *Harvey's Bristol Cream* and read or chat. Sometimes, Christina would come over with the grands and they'd take trips to Hyde Park.

Winnie wonders how they can rekindle that spirit of togetherness. She decides to cut back on some of her activities. She now goes with him to the beach when she can. She even carries the pails of water for him, so they can build the sandcastles together—especially for the competition coming up next week. She still cannot understand his preoccupation.

"Why you spend so much time building this elaborate sandcastle for the tide to just come and wash it away in a day or so?"

"Oh, I'll just build another one."

Three young women walk by and pause to admire Lionel's creation. He beams with pride.

A flicker of annoyance crosses Winnie's face.

"I'm talking to you and you wallowing in the little pissin tail gals' praise."

"So what you saying now?"

"Before me forget, you steal away things from my kitchen—my best set of measuring spoons, spatula and the melon baller that I use to make my fruit baskets."

"Cho!" he expels the word in one breath. He holds the spatula at an angle and cuts into the sand with a sawing motion. He uses her measuring spoon to clear away the excess sand from the window ledge he is carving. "You see this?" he said, rocking back on his heels. "I never build these fancy turrets in the other ones. Every day now I get to try something new."

"So what's next then?"

"I am going to try building a moat after this."

She chuckles despite herself. "You ever hear the saying, "no fool like an old fool?""

He gives her a mysterious smile. "You think mi old…"

At that moment, the sand shifts beneath Winnie's feet. She falls to the ground on her knees. She struggles to regain her balance, sighing resignedly when he didn't even notice.

In the ensuing months, Winnie tries hard to keep up with her charities and pay more attention to her husband. But on Ash Wednesday, the unthinkable happens.

Lionel gets sick and Winnie rushes him to the hospital.

"Just a little polyp," the doctor says. "…a touch of cancer, we'll have to operate."

Winnie, grateful for this reprieve that Lionel is not going to be taken from her just yet, doubles up on her attention to him.

She pours the pumpkin soup in the enamel carrier with little pieces of dasheen in it and turkey neck. It surprises her that he is actually ill. Ever since they left England, Lionel's been on such a health kick.

He would say to her: "Me no want no whole heap of food in my soup. Don't bother with the dumplings."

"Eh, eh what is this—since when you don't want food in your soup?"

"You nuh see how me belly a get flat?" He would pose in front of her, flexing his muscles.

Winnie smiles as she remembers that conversation.

Lionel had the surgery yesterday and will leave the hospital in a few days. She walks down the hospital corridor with the carrier of soup in one hand, and a tote bag filled with *Men's Health*, *GQ*, *Time* and *The Economist*, in her other hand.

As she approaches the room, she hears his deep rumbling laughter, as only Lionel can laugh, straight from his belly.

Good, he has visitors. That will put him in a good mood. She pushes the door open.

There on his bed, perches a young woman about 28 years old. She wears a curly, jet black weave cascading down her forehead and way down her back. She swings a baby girl from side-to-side in front of Lionel's face. He tickles the baby's toes.

Winnie says to herself, "Oh she favor his god-daughter. What a way she turn big woman and have baby too." Winnie pastes a big smile on her face.

"Lionel, you look good today man. And who are your visitors?"

Lionel's eyes suddenly shift to track the stripes in the bed sheet. His Adam's Apple bops up and down. His mouth opens like a fish gasping for air but nothing comes out.

Winnie's eyes dart to the girl then to the baby. A bolt of recognition rips through her body.

The baby looks exactly like Christina at the same age.

The girl raises her chin, a self-satisfied "ketch you" smile tugging at the corners of her mouth.

"Lionel." Winnie calls out his name, sounding like the mew of a wounded cat. "What's going on?"

she asks, her voice rising to a hissy pitch. Her knees wobble and she holds on to the back of a chair for support. All the time her eyes flick from Lionel, to the girl, to the baby.

Silence. A silence deep and loud. In the far reaches of Winnie's mind, the familiar sound of the surf crashes in, clogging her ears and flooding her senses. She hears a steady hum. As the surf recedes, she realizes the hum is coming from the girl underneath the pile of weave:

> *Rock-a-bye baby in the tree top,*
> *when the wind blows the cradle will*
> *rock.*
> *Rock.*
> *Rock.*
> *Rock.*

Mother to Son

Earnest come into de room and shet de door. Nuh fret 'bout your company outside, Eulalee will give dem a bottle of peach aerated water dat you bring from farrin. When dat finish, dey can drink coc'nut water. But bwoy we 'ave to have a little talk. Come sit down on the bed. Me can't talk loud mek no body hear—me have to whisper this:

Bwoy...is five years since you left for farrin and you come back same way? No little haccent, no little lingo?

Bwoy...me shame a you until me don't know how to face de people on de verandah. Look pon your clothes!

Bwoy...not even a silk pleat front trousers? Not even a black face watch wit' the diamon' at 12:00 o'clock? Or even a circular phone to stick out your back pocket? Wha meck you dry so?

Me say, when de mini-bus drop you at de gate an you turn your head and smile, every man, woman and chile crane dem neck to peep in your mouth. Me look an' shet me eye, for...is de same white teeth you left here wit'.

Bwoy...not even one gold teet to ketch de glitter from de sun?

Me shame a you cyan done!

Yessiday when you pick de mango from de tree and suck…an de juice run down de back of your han' —to your helbow. Me shet me eye again…because me remember when Bredda T son came home from farrin, and you know? While him playing dominoes wit his friend dem under the guango tree, me say, him took out a leetle plastic bag. In it was plenty of dried mango strips —and it was from farrin farrin! All de men dem look at each odder and shake dem head, for dem never see such class.

Bwoy…you see? Dat is refinement!

To save face in de district, me gwine to have to beg you a favor. For Gawd's sake, show dem dat little Merican rub off pon you. When me call you again, do, don't answer "yes mummy," you hear? Go down in your troat and say "yeah mawma" just like dey do on *Fresh Prince of Bel'Air*.

When people aks you a question, mi dear, don't hanswer dem directly, lean forward little bit in your chair…pretend dere is clothes pin on your nose and say "haw?"

Inspired by Louise Bennett's poem "No Lickle Twang"

ACKNOWLEDGEMENTS

Thanks to my sisters—Authrine Rose, Thelma Rose-Barrett, and Linnette DaCosta for being the bedrock of all my creative endeavors. And especially to my brother, Douglas Rose, for being an integral part of my childhood. To my older brother, Victor Rose, my parents—Walpole and Hermine Rose—the memories live on, and I'm forever grateful.

A great big thank you to my creative team, Naomi Skarzinski and Verone Johnston for dotting the "i's" and crossing the "t's"; Mark Steven Weinberger and Aeron Cargill for implementing my vision.

I'm grateful to Andre Claxton, Andrew Roblin, Jenifa Laidlaw, and Val Timoll for their feedback and unwavering support.

A-Z GLOSSARY
OF WORDS AND PHRASES USED IN
THE CONTEXT OF THIS WORK

Bangarang	Noise, uproar, disturbance.
Body come down	Rectal prolapse.
Bumbo	An expletive, literally meaning, "a person's bottom". Considered the ultimate swear word when paired with "claat" and "rass" or "hole".
Chigger Foot	When referred to a person it means dirt poor. It's derived from the fact that slaves would get infested with chiggers as they rarely wore shoes.
Callaloo	A dark, green leafy vegetable, like spinach.
Chimmy	Chamber pot.
Chiney bumps	Hair is parted in a variety of geometric shapes, twisted and rolled into bumps. The name is derived from the bump-like fasteners on Chinese clothing. Today, the official term in the diaspora is Nubian knots or Bantu knots.
Cho	Mild expletive reflecting annoyance or impatience.

Cotta	A wad of cloth or leaves to protect the head from heavy loads. Example: The person carries a bunch of bananas or a large bucket of water resting on the cotta on his head.
Cutting ten	Crossing legs at the knee—with the ankle touching the knee of the other leg.
Cyaan	Cannot.
Dawg	'Dog' is the literal translation in Jamaica. "Whassup Dawg" or "Wuddup Dawg" is an urban-inspired form of affectionate greeting among African Americans. The slang word, "dawg" is used to replace the person's name.
Duppy	Spirit of the dead or ghost.
Dutchie	Heavy, round-bottomed cooking pot.
Farrin	Foreign—usually U.S., Canada, U.K.
Guzu	Obeah
Kananga water	A cologne based on the essential oil of Ylang Ylang, produced by the British on plantations in Jamaica in the 19th Century. It's used for various rituals including spiritual cleansing and appeasing dead spirits.
Kin puppa lick	Somersault.

Leaf-a-Life	The Leaf of Life plant is derived from Africa. The leaf is used to cure abscesses, sores and headaches. The tea is used for colds, asthma, kidney stones, ulcers and more.
Nutten no go so	It's not true.
Nyam	To eat. Example: "Let's go nyam some jerk pork."
Ooonu	You all.
Pickney	Any child. Also means your own child or even an adult son or daughter.
Pissin tail	An upstart. One who doesn't know his or her place.
Quashie	Peasant. No pedigree.
Rass	A common swear word used to intensify the meaning of words. Example: It's rass hot! See also the meaning of 'bumbo'.
Sangster bills	Jamaican hundred dollar bills with photo of Sir Donald Sangster, former prime minister.
Sankey	Revival or evangelical songs collected in a 'hymn book' which are sung at special events (i.e. funerals). Named after Ira B. Sankey (British), the Salvation

Army popularized this form of singing in Jamaica. The Sankey songs include hand-clapping, tambourines, body movements and rhythmic singing.

Senseh fowl	Fowls used to unearth 'guzu' or obeah planted with the intent to harm the occupants of the home. The fowls also chase mongoose from eating crops.
Sibble orange	A rough, thick-skinned, sour orange used to make lemonade and marmalade. Official name— Seville orange.
Sky Juice	A clear plastic bag filled with shaved/crushed ice and fruit flavored syrups poured over the ice.
Smaddy	Somebody.
Sorrel	A red Christmas drink.
Tie-head	Head scarf.
Tittivate	Preening in front of a mirror.
White marl	Limestone.

ABOUT THE AUTHOR

Lena Joy Rose is author of the historical romance, *Escape to Falmouth*, co-author of a nonfiction, and publisher/ CEO of Minna Press.

When not writing or working on her business, Lena enjoys reading historical fiction/romance, multicultural stories, travelling to foreign countries and learning about people.

Lena is also an active board member of the Georgian Society of Jamaica and resides in both Jamaica and North Carolina.

Contact the author at lena@minnapress.com or join her mailing list at www.minnapress.com

OTHER WORKS

Escape to Falmouth
Minna Press, 2010

How to Say it: Marketing with New Media
(co-author)
Penguin/Prentice Hall Press, 2008

Escape from Falmouth
(scheduled for release soon)
Minna Press